BERTIE THE BE

Story by
BARBARA HAYES

Illustrated by J.B. Long

OCTOPUS BOOKS

A RIDGMOUNT BOOK
First published 1986 by Octopus Books Ltd
59 Grosvenor Street, London W1

© 1986 Martspress Ltd
ISBN: 0 7064 2592 8

Produced by Mandarin Publishers Ltd
22a Westlands Road
Quarry Bay, Hong Kong

Printed in Hong Kong

Bertie the Bentley was as happy as a car could be. He had a kind owner who took him on lots of interesting jaunts. Then when war came life changed suddenly – for the worse! This is the story of how Bertie narrowly misses the scrap yard and goes on to save a man's life!

Bertie the Bentley was brand new, and very powerful. His great headlamps glared from either side of his face. His foglight stood at the ready between two black horns. Bertie was big and tough, but he was patient and even-tempered too. He was a fine car.

Jimmy Taylor was looking for a new car. He walked into the London Car Show Rooms where Bertie stood, shiny and eager to go.

'That is the car for me,' said Mister Taylor to the salesman. 'I like his style.'

So started the long friendship between Jimmy Taylor, who was a clever engineer, and Bertie the Bentley.

'You're coming to a good home, Bentley my lad,' smiled Jimmy, as he drove Bertie through the green English countryside to a pretty, stone house on a busy country road.

Bertie was pleased to see a garage next to his new home. 'That's handy for servicing,' he thought, not realizing the garage belonged to his new owner.

Life was wonderful for Bertie the Bentley in those early years. Living next door to a busy garage was fun. There were always plenty of other cars to chat to, and Bertie himself was regularly serviced and maintained and cleaned. Jimmy saw to that.

Several times a year, Bertie would be taken on holiday, quite often to somewhere in Europe, with Jimmy and his friend, Fruity Frobisher. Best of all, Bertie liked the long straight tree-lined avenues of France, where he could get up a really good speed.

The greatest fun Bertie had in those carefree far-off days was to go on car rallies. With Jimmy driving and Fruity Frobisher map reading, Bertie had to find his way at a steady speed over strange roads to distant checkpoints. He always arrived at exactly the correct time and in perfect condition.

Then finally, Bertie would have to do speed tests over mountain roads and round hairpin bends.

'What a magnificent, steady car,' the people would gasp as Bertie went by – usually to win, of course!

After winning one very important car rally, Bertie drove through the streets of a town in France with Jimmy Taylor sitting up on the back waving a bottle of champagne at the crowds of cheering people.

'This is wonderful!' thought Bertie, 'I'm sure I don't know why anyone is *ever* miserable. Life is a *grand affair*.'

It was really easy for Bertie to be steadfast and strong, while he was being so well treated!

'Thank you! Thank you!' he beamed at the crowds.

To tell the truth, Bertie was becoming rather spoiled. It was only his natural good nature and steady character which saved him from becoming unbearable.

'Oh yes, well, I usually *do* win, actually!' he would remark to other cars – and they could hardly accuse him of boasting, because he was telling the truth.

Wherever they went, Jimmy always saw that Bertie spent the night in a warm garage and was well cleaned.

'Quite right!' Bertie would think. 'I deserve it in return for being so reliable.'

The years went happily by and one summer, Bertie noticed that a young lady named Pam was coming for rather a lot of drives with Jimmy and himself. Pam was very nice and Bertie was pleased when Jimmy announced that he was going to marry her.

On the day of the wedding, Bertie dashed to and fro between the house and the church, taking everyone where they wanted to go.

'How would they ever manage without me?' thought Bertie, looking proudly across at the wedding party.

Then one day their happiness was sadly interrupted.

'War has been declared, Bentley old pal,' said Jimmy in a serious voice. 'There will be no more petrol for the likes of you, no more holidays, no more rallies, just lots of worry for all of us.'

He drained Bentley's engine, took off his tyres and stood him up on bricks in the garage.

'This must all be a dreadful mistake!' gasped Bertie, who did not really understand the meaning of war. 'This can't be happening to a successful car like *me*!'

A few days later, Pam and Jimmy came out wearing strange khaki-coloured clothes. 'We have joined the army,' explained Jimmy. 'We must go away to help in the war. You will have to be patient and wait here until we return.'

Bertie watched as Pam and Jimmy stood in the gateway of their home, waving goodbye.

'How long will they be gone?' he wondered. 'How long shall I have to stay here all by myself? How long do wars last?' There was no one to answer him.

Poor Bertie was feeling really sorry for himself, when suddenly he heard footsteps and a cheery voice. Looking round, he saw Jimmy's old Auntie Winnie.

'Well, Bertie my boy,' she smiled. 'I am going to keep an eye on you and the house while Pam and Jimmy are away. I don't know anything about cars, but I'm all you've got, so make the best of me.'

Bertie began to feel more cheerful and managed a little smile. Perhaps things would not be so bad!

Auntie Winnie closed the garage for the night.

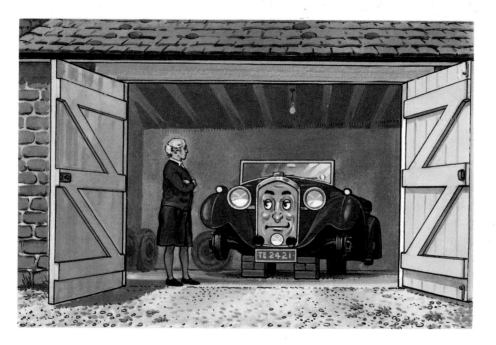

At first things weren't too bad. Auntie Winnie looked in every day, gave Bertie a dust and stayed for a little chat. But gradually she became too busy with her own work to bother.

One of the panes of glass in the garage window broke. Leaves and dirt blew in. A family of birds nested on top of one of Bertie's black horns.

'I want to be useful,' he sighed, 'but how can I be while I am shut up in here? I wish Jimmy and Pam would come home.'

Then one day, the garage doors were opened and the sun came shining in. Blinking in the bright light, Bertie saw Auntie Winnie with an old gentleman.

'This is the car, Doctor Goodheart,' said Auntie Winnie. 'I'm sure Jimmy will not mind if you use it. We all have to do our bit in wartime, even Bertie.'

Bertie's heart leapt. Did this mean he would be taken out of the garage and put back on the road again? He did hope so.

'I will try him,' said Doctor Goodheart.

'Wonderful!' gasped Bertie, feeling happier and happier, as his tyres were put back on. Then he was rolled out into the fresh air and oil and petrol were poured into his engine. Special shades were fitted over all his lamps, so he could hardly be seen after dark.

All the proper mechanics had gone away to the war and only the apprentice, Tommy, was left to service Bertie's engine. He did not know how to do it properly, but Bertie did not complain. He was so happy to be working again. Why worry about a few loose screws?

'Now, Bertie my lad,' said Doctor Goodheart, 'my old car is worn out and I need you to drive me round to visit my patients. A doctor's work is very important and I rely on you not to let me down.'

'I won't,' vowed Bertie, and in spite of the bad servicing he started bravely and drove steadily round the country lanes, never complaining for a moment about the aches and pains caused by the rattling screws.

It was so good to be out again, and to see children playing in the cottage gardens.

Usually Doctor Goodheart looked after sick people in the village, but sometimes, when there was an air-raid on the nearby town, he was called in to help. Then, he would fetch Bertie from his garage and they would drive through the night, lit up only by search lights and by the flames of burning houses.

Even though Bertie ached and grated from bad servicing and poor oil, he would start up and drive steadfastly through the cold night. He had enjoyed the good times. Now he must help in the bad times!

However, the day came at last when even a car as brave and strong as Bertie could no longer fight against all the wrong things that had been done to him.

'WHEEE! WHIRRRR! CHOKE! GASP!'

No matter how Bertie heaved and struggled, he could not start. Doctor Goodheart sat in the driving seat pulling and pushing at every knob and lever he could see, in an effort to get Bertie going.

'Eeeeek! Ouch! Stop! That hurts!' shrieked Bertie. '*Please* send for a mechanic!'

By that time even young Tommy had gone off to the war.

'Heaven help the army if Tommy is servicing their cars,' thought Bertie.

The only mechanic left in the village was Mister Oilygrin. He was a good mechanic all right, but he was not an honest man. Bertie did not like the look of him when he arrived at the garage.

'Try to get this car started for me, please,' said the Doctor, pointing at Bertie.

Doctor Goodheart went off to make a phone call and Mister Oilygrin lifted Bertie's bonnet. He smiled his horrible oily grin.

'Why, what a magnificent car,' he muttered. 'Nothing wrong with it that proper treatment won't put right. But I will tell the Doctor it is useless.'

Bertie the Bentley could hardly believe his ears. If he was a magnificent car with nothing wrong with him, why should Mister Oilygrin say he was useless?

Mister Oilygrin shut Bertie's bonnet and laughed.

When Doctor Goodheart came back from making his phone call, Mister Oilygrin told him: 'This Bentley is all worn out, doctor. You had better find another car. I will put him back up on his bricks and leave him for Mister Taylor to get rid of at the end of the war.'

'Oh dear! What a nuisance! Well, thank you for your help, Mister Oilygrin,' said Doctor Goodheart, who knew nothing about car engines.

Bertie had never felt so puzzled. Why was Mister Oilygrin telling such lies? He soon found out!

As soon as the doctor was out of the way, Mister Oilygrin re-opened Bertie's bonnet. 'Now,' he chuckled, rubbing his hands and grinning to himself, 'I will take all the best parts from this engine and make lots of money selling them as spare parts. By the time Jimmy Taylor returns home and discovers what has happened, I shall be far away.'

He did as he said and once more Bertie was left in the care of Auntie Winnie, who had no idea of the terrible thing that had happened.

Bertie spent month after lonely month in the cold garage. In the old days it had been easy for him always to be cheerful and happy. But now it needed all his strength of character not to get downhearted. All he could do was to wait, and be brave and hopeful and patient.

Then, one day, Bertie heard the sound of boots crunching on the ground of the yard outside. The garage doors were flung open and in strode Jimmy Taylor. The war was over!

'It's great to see you, Bentley my lad,' grinned Jimmy. 'Goodness knows when we shall ever get any petrol for a run out, but let's have a look at you. I don't believe all this nonsense Auntie Winnie is talking, about you being unreliable and broken down.' He opened Bertie's bonnet and gasped in amazement.

'Someone has taken half your parts away,' he said. 'Why it must have been that rascal, Oilygrin!'

He patted Bertie kindly on the bonnet.

'Don't worry. I'll put you right again,' he said.

Bertie slept more happily that night than he had done for months. He knew that now Jimmy was back, his troubles were over.

A few days later Jimmy's wife Pam also returned home from the war. She laughed when she saw Jimmy out in the yard, surrounded by tools and grease and rags and with his head tucked under Bertie's bonnet.

'It didn't take you two long to get back together again,' she said. But it was many months before Jimmy could find all the parts needed to make Bertie fit.

However, at last the great day came when Bertie was well enough to go on a long run.

'My brother, Sir Smiley Smoothdeal, has written to invite us to spend Christmas with him at Whiteporch Manor,' said Pam. 'He is goodnatured and works very hard to keep the old family house going. Let's drive Bertie down to stay with him.'

So, as daylight was fading, Bertie, Jimmy and Pam found themselves on the long driveway leading to Whiteporch Manor.

Many years later, Jimmy and Pam and Bertie would all come to live at Whiteporch, but they did not dream of that yet. Pam's brother was waiting for them at the porch, which was all decorated with pretty coloured lights ready for Christmas.

'Welcome,' said Sir Smiley, 'my son, Alec, is waiting inside to say "hello" to his Aunt and Uncle.'

He pointed at Bertie. 'Surely you're not still using that old wreck!' he laughed. 'It's time you bought a new car. That one should go to the scrap yard.'

Bertie felt very hurt – and worried too. He was getting old. He might not be as fit as he used to be, especially after all his troubles. Perhaps it was selfish of him to want to go on driving round with Jimmy and Pam. Perhaps they *should* have a younger car!

Jimmy put Bertie away in a warm garage with a cosy oil heater, and wrapped a tartan blanket over his bonnet.

That night it snowed and it snowed. The telephone lines were all weighed down and stopped working.

Sleeping snugly in his warm garage, Bertie knew nothing of the bad weather until, in the small hours of the morning, Jimmy came running in, dragging on his overcoat. 'Wake up, Bentley!' he called. 'We're in trouble and I reckon you are the only car that can help. Sir Smiley has fallen ill and must go to hospital. The phones aren't working and there's deep snow everywhere. Someone has to get through it to take him to a doctor.'

Bertie struggled to wake up.

'Now is the time to show I can be as strong and trustworthy as I was in my youth,' thought Bertie.

He roared his engine into life, blazed out with all his lights, swept up his hood to keep out the snow, and drove with Jimmy to the front of Whiteporch.

Poor Sir Smiley, wrapped in a blanket, was carried out to Bertie's back seat.

'Don't worry,' smiled Jimmy. 'Bertie and I will get you through. There isn't a more reliable car than my old Bentley. The snow won't worry him.'

Even for a great-hearted car like Bertie, the weather was fearsome. The snow lay so thickly on the ground, it was difficult to see where the road ended and the fields began.

Bertie dreaded that at any moment he might lurch into a ditch and be unable to get out again. The icy wind tried to freeze Bertie's engine into silence. The snow slithered under his wheels.

'I will *not* let Jimmy down! I *will* get through,' vowed Bertie, gripping the road and rolling on.

At last they reached the hospital and Sir Smiley was carefully helped inside.

Jimmy Taylor turned to pat his faithful Bertie on the bonnet. 'You got us here!' he said. 'I *knew* you would. There will never be another car like you. We will stay together always.'

Bertie felt so proud! Thanks to his efforts the doctors were able to save Sir Smiley's life and reunite him with his family in time for them all to have a very happy Christmas.

Other books in the series:

MICKY THE MG
Cheeky Micky the MG is bought by a collector of classic cars. Join him in his scrapes with Richard the Rolls and the short-tempered Sir 'Smart' Alec Smoothdeal.

FREDDY THE FORD
Fortunate Freddy the Ford is rescued from a hire car's life of drudgery by a rich adventurer. Join them on their exciting escapades in exotic locations around the world.

MAURICE MINOR
Maurice Minor moves to town. Meet his new friends and join him on a chaotic camping trip as he saves his young owner from a soaking at the seaside.